ORCHARD BOOKS
96 Leonard Street, London EC2A 4XD
Orchard Books Australia
32/45-51 Huntley Street, Alexandria, NSW 2015
ISBN 1 84362 276 9 (hardback)
ISBN 1 84362 278 5 (paperback)
First published in Great Britain in 2003
First paperback publication in 2004
Text © Sandra Glover 2003
Illustrations © Gary Parsons 2003
The rights of Sandra Glover to be identified as the author
and of Gary Parsons to be identified as the illustrator of this
work have been asserted by them in accordance with the
Copyright, Designs and Patents Act, 1988.
A CIP catalogue record for this book is available
from the British Library.
1 3 5 7 9 10 8 6 4 2 (hardback)
1 3 5 7 9 10 8 6 4 2 (paperback)
Printed in Great Britain

MONKEY-MAN

SANDRA GLOVER
Illustrated by Garry Parsons

ORCHARD BOOKS

CHAPTER 1

"Maxwell Jordan, what am I going to do with you?" my teacher often asks.

Sometimes she's talking about my behaviour. Not that I'm badly behaved, you understand. Just unlucky. Things have a nasty habit of going wrong for me, as you'll see.

At other times, she's talking about my work.

"Max, what have I told you about stories?" she moans. "They should have a beginning, a middle and an end. Preferably in that order!"

Well, fine. I expect she's right. But this is my own true story and it's not for school, so I'm going to start it in the middle. With the terrible scream in the night...

I'd been having this fantastic dream where I'd just scored the winning goal for England in the World Cup Final and the crowd was going wild. So, naturally, I thought the scream was coming from them. Until it started to sink in that it was the wrong sort of scream entirely.

I rubbed my eyes. The goal post disappeared. The players disappeared. The crowd disappeared. But the scream was still there.

No wonder it had woken me up! A scream like that could wake the dead. Could be coming from the dead, for all

I knew. It sounded like every ghost, ghoul, spook and phantom, from every graveyard in the country, had suddenly decided to meet on our front lawn to have a nice long wail about their woes.

OK, so maybe I'm exaggerating. But only a bit.

I leapt out of bed, stumbled towards the door, barged out onto the landing and crashed into a horrible, shadowy figure.

"That's my foot, you great lump," said the figure, elbowing me in the ribs.

The snappy voice told me it was my sister, Kerry.

"Sorry," I muttered, switching on the light. "What's going on?"

"How should I know?" Kerry snapped, as we headed downstairs. "Sounds like someone's being murdered."

"Hang on," I said, grabbing my sister's arm, as she went to open the front door. "If someone's being murdered, maybe we should just stay..."

Too late. Kerry was already outside. As was half the neighbourhood. It was amazingly light out there, with the street lamps on and the full moon beaming like a spotlight on some bizarre fashion show – Mr Sharif in his stripy pyjamas. Sally Thomas tugging at a very short nightdress. Old Mr Peters, whose wrinkly face seemed to have collapsed without his false teeth. And Nick Leech, who likes to act dead hard, looking ridiculous in an old *Batman* T-shirt, hanging round his knobbly knees.

In the middle of it all was our next-door neighbour, Mrs Burrows, still screaming, as more and more people gathered round.

"Calm down, Brenda," said Mrs Thomas, putting her arm round her.

"But I saw it," she squealed. "It was horrible. Horrible! Call the police! Call the police!"

Half a dozen people immediately pulled mobiles from their dressing-gown pockets. Honestly, they must sleep with them under their pillows or something!

"Hang on!" I said. "She was probably just having a nightmare or something."

"And my poor Poppet," Mrs Burrows wailed. "What has it done with my Poppet?"

"Sit down," said Mr Thomas, taking off his dressing gown and spreading it out on the low garden wall. "There, that's better. Now just tell us what happened. Nice and calmly."

"I heard Poppet barking and scratching at the front door," said Brenda Burrows. "I thought she wanted to go out. She's very good, like that, is Poppet. Never makes a mess in the house. Always wakes me up if she wants a tiddly-diddle."

Tiddly-diddle, I ask you! You'd think Mrs Burrows was an infant, the way she talks sometimes, instead of a grown woman of sixty-two!

"So, I opened the door. And there it was," she shrieked, pointing in the direction of our front lawn. "Staring at me over the fence."

"There *what* was?" said Mr Thomas.

"The THING!" she said, shuddering. "Ooh, it was horrible, it was. All huge and hairy. Well, Poppet took one look and shot off round the back with the great hairy thing lurching after her. Ooh, my poor, poor, Poppet."

"Er, so what exactly was it like?" said my sister, Kerry, edging forward.

"Oh, for goodness sake," I hissed. "Don't encourage her!"

"Like a...like a...Yeti or giant ape," Brenda said. "Covered in long, reddish hair. With huge, mad, glinting eyes.

About seven foot tall. Wearing nothing but a pair of baggy shorts."

"No it wasn't!" I said, as everyone turned to stare at me.

CHAPTER 2

"Did you see it then, Max?" asked Nick Leech.

"Er...no," I said. "I mean, I couldn't have done, could I? Because it wasn't there, was it? It's obvious. Mrs Burrows was still half asleep. She dreamt it. She imagined it."

"And I suppose Poppet imagined it too, did she?" Brenda Burrows snapped.

"She probably shot off after our cat, as usual," I said.

"That was no cat!" Brenda yelled. "I know a cat when I see one, thank you very much. They're not seven foot tall, and they don't lope around on their hind legs!"

Seven foot, I thought, doing a rough calculation. That's more than two metres! Ridiculous. "Well, maybe it was just a very tall tramp or something," I said.

But no one was listening. A police car had just pulled up and two cops

were getting out. A youngish lady and an older bloke.

"Now then," said the policeman. "What's going on?"

Cops must be specially trained to listen to twenty people at once because he seemed to be taking it all in while the lady was scribbling down notes.

Eventually the noise died down. I could tell by the look on the policeman's face that he didn't believe Mrs Burrows. Who would, with a crazy story like that?

But then Mr Sharif, who lives on the other side of us, chipped in.

"You know, it's funny," he said. "Because when I got up to go to the loo last night, I was sure there was someone prowling about..."

"And did you tell Mrs Burrows about this, by any chance?" I asked.

"I think I might have mentioned it this afternoon, yes."

"Well, it's obvious then, isn't it?" I said. "She must have been worrying about it before she went to sleep and dreamt up the ape thing!"

"Real little detective, aren't you?" said the policeman, smiling at me.

I beamed back at him, relieved that it had all been sorted so easily.

"OK," he said. "I suggest everyone locks up carefully and gets back to bed while we have a quick look."

"You kids, particularly," said the

policewoman, looking at us. "Are your parents around?"

"We live with Dad," said Kerry.

"And your dad is?" asked the policewoman, as if looking round for a likely candidate.

"In bed," said Kerry. "With a broken leg....fell off a ladder when he was painting the kitchen ceiling."

"Oh dear," said the policewoman. "Well, I'd better come in with you. Just in case."

"No, it's OK," I said, yawning. "No one could have got in. 'Especially as there was never anyone in the first place."

"Yes there was!" shrieked Brenda. "I told you! A big hairy monkey-man! And it's eaten my Poppet!"

"No it hasn't, Mrs B," said Nick Leech, who'd been crawling around under a bush. "I've got her, look!"

He lifted something up. And, if I hadn't known, I'd never have guessed it was Mrs Burrow's Yorkshire Terrier. It looked more like a hedgehog that had been sitting on an electric fence for a couple of days. A writhing mass of spiky hair.

"Oooh, my poor, poor, Poppet," Brenda Burrows screamed as Kerry and I made our escape.

We darted inside and locked the door.

"I'd better go and check on Dad," Kerry said. "Just in case…"

"Right," I said. "Good idea! I'm just going to grab a drink."

A cold draught hit me as soon as I walked into the kitchen and in the darkness, I could see a pale curtain moving.

As I edged towards the light switch,

20

my foot touched something warm and furry.

"Yowwwwwwwww."

The inhuman screech brought Kerry clattering back downstairs, just as I'd turned on the light.

"Er, I think I trod on the cat," I said.

"You certainly did, you great clumsy oik," said Kerry, going over to stroke Marmalade, who was standing on the kitchen table, his back arched and his ginger tail all fluffed up.

"I didn't know he was in," I said. "I'm sure I let him out before I went to bed."

"You did," said Kerry, shivering. "But the back door's open, look."

Well, that explained the draught and the moving curtain.

"Maybe it blew open," I said. "Or maybe..."

We stared at each other for a moment, both thinking the same thing.

"Have you seen Dad, yet?" I said.

"Not yet," said Kerry. "I didn't get the chance with you clowning around down here. I'll go now."

"OK, I'll lock up."

Have you noticed how cats bear grudges? Marmalade does, anyway. No way was he going to let me put him out. He wouldn't let me near him! So I left him, hissing and spitting, on the table and bolted the door.

"Max!" Kerry shouted from upstairs. "Max, come here, quick."

I followed the direction of her voice to Dad's room, and stared at the crumpled duvet and the otherwise empty bed.

"He's not here," Kerry said.

"I can see that!"

"You don't think..."

She suddenly paused, nudging me,

nodding in the direction of the wardrobe – the large, walk-in wardrobe, with one of the doors ever so slightly open. In the gap, I could see one of dad's suits hanging, and hear the faint rustle of something moving towards us.

I followed the direction of Kerry's eyes, down, down to the bottom of the wardrobe. To a glimpse of feet. Large, dark, hairy, feet.

CHAPTER 3

Kerry breathed a loud sigh of relief.

"It's all right, Dad," she said. "You can come out now."

The door creaked opened and out shuffled Brenda's 'monkey-man'. Tall, but not seven foot! Reddish hair. No mad, staring eyes. In fact, you could hardly see any eyes at all through all the hair. But otherwise he was pretty much as poor Brenda had described. Very, very hairy!

"It's not all right, though, is it?" I snapped, looking from Kerry to the monkey-man. "I told you not to risk going out again, Dad!"

"I can't stay cooped up in here forever," Dad grumbled.

"It won't be forever," I pointed out. "Just until..."

"Feels like forever," moaned Dad. "I just wanted some fresh air. I thought I'd be safe enough at three o'clock in the morning! How was I to know Brenda Burrows was going to let her dog out. Yappy little thing! And her in that long white nightie with those stupid rollers sticking out of her head. Gave me a right shock, it did."

"Not as bad as the shock you gave her!" said Kerry, laughing.

"It's not funny," I said. "And you'll have to be more careful, Dad. We can't keep covering up for you. I think I

managed to convince everyone that Brenda Burrows was just dreaming, but we've had the police snooping round!"

"I know," said Dad. "That's why I slipped in through the back door and hid."

"Hid!" I said. "It wouldn't exactly take Sherlock Holmes to find you, would it? With your great, ugly toes poking out!"

"Leave him alone," Kerry snapped, rushing over and throwing her arms round him. "He's not ugly! And don't you forget, Max...this was all your stupid fault in the first place."

"Oh, right!" I said. "That's typical, that is! Blame me for everything!"

I stomped out and stormed back to bed. But I couldn't sleep. The trouble was that Kerry was right, in a way. It was my fault. But I hadn't meant anything terrible to happen. I hadn't meant to cause Dad any trouble. Quite the opposite, in fact.

It had all started about a month earlier, when I was trying to think of something special to buy Dad for his thirty-fifth birthday. Kerry had already got hers bought and wrapped. Socks and some pens for work. I mean how boring can you get?

But buying presents for Dad isn't easy. And if you ask him, all he ever says is, "Oh, don't bother buying me anything. I've got you two, haven't I? What more could I possibly want?"

Sounds soppy, I know, but he means it!

So I was really struggling, which is why I read the Futurama catalogue that came through the door. "Great gifts!" it announced. "Get tomorrow's inventions today!"

Most of it was rubbish. Couldn't imagine Dad needing a musical corkscrew and the electric nail-clippers looked positively dangerous. The alarm clock in the shape of a fat bottom, which woke you up by making a rude noise, looked quite funny but then Dad doesn't always share my sense of humour.

I'd almost given up, when I spotted something nestled between *Herbal Relief for Embarrassing Itches* and *Chocolate Scented Bath Gel.*

Why hadn't I thought of it before? Hair restorer. The perfect gift for the man who has everything...except hair!

Poor Dad had been bald for as long as I could remember, though I know he had hair when I was born, 'cos I've seen the photos. But then, seven years ago, when Mum was killed in a car accident, he lost the lot. Just like that. Stress-related Alopecia, the doctor said it was.

Kerry, who was five when Mum

died, reckons she remembers Dad's hair falling out in handfuls. I don't, though, 'cos I was only two. I don't even remember my mum really, which upsets me sometimes.

Anyway, Dad reckoned he didn't mind being bald. Said it makes him look distinguished. But I wasn't sure. And I couldn't help wondering whether that was the reason he'd never had a girlfriend or anything.

He's a good-looking guy, my dad. Quite intelligent, for a teacher, and a good laugh, when you get him in the right mood. So how come nobody seemed to fancy him?

"Oh, I've had my chances!" Dad laughed, when I'd tried to talk to him about it, one day. "But...I don't know... I guess I've just never met the right person."

It was an excuse, I was sure. And

surely he'd feel more attractive and confident about himself if he had a full head of hair again? Of course he would. My gift idea was brilliant. Absolutely brilliant.

CHAPTER 4

So that was it. I sent off for the hair restorer. It wasn't cheap, either. Two months' pocket money it cost me!

Which is why I wasn't too pleased when, after a fortnight, nothing had arrived.

"What do you expect?" sneered Kerry. "From a dodgy catalogue. You'd better give them a ring."

Only I couldn't, could I? Because, by then, I'd lost the catalogue, hadn't I?

Luckily, or perhaps unluckily, as it turned out, the parcel arrived on the Friday morning of Dad's birthday. Just in time for me to shove a bit of fancy wrapping paper round it and hand it over.

"Just what I needed!" said Dad, opening Kerry's boring offering. "Socks and pens. Brill, Kerry! Thank you."

He pulled the wrapping paper off my gift, held up the plastic bottle and burst out laughing.

"*Dr Hepplewaite's Hair Restorer,*" he chortled, looking round, as if to see where his real present was. As if my carefully thought out and VERY expensive gift was a joke!

"You are going to try it, aren't you, Dad?" I said, as the smile rapidly disappeared from his face. "I mean, it's not a joke."

"Of course I'll try it, Max!" he said, rubbing the top of his shiny head.

"I hope it's got a money-back guarantee," giggled Kerry. "'Cos there's not a chance of it working."

It seemed as though my irritating sister might be right for once. Over the weekend, I kept staring at Dad's head for signs of growth. Not a single strand. Not a hint of a hair.

On Monday morning, I ran my hand over his head while he was having breakfast, in the hope of feeling a bit of spiky stubble. Nothing. It was as smooth and bald as the boiled egg he was eating.

"Yes, er, well," said Dad. "You wouldn't expect it to work immediately, would you?"

"No, you wouldn't expect it to work!" I told him that night, confronting him with the unopened bottle. "Not if you don't even bother to use it!"

"I'm sorry, Max," he said. "I mean, it was thoughtful of you and everything but I've sort of got used to being bald. It might look a bit silly if I suddenly start sprouting bits of hair."

"You won't know if you don't even try," I moaned.

"I will try it, Max," Dad said. "I promise."

"When?"

"Soon."

"Tonight," I said.

"Go on, Dad," said Kerry. "You may as well give it a go. It'll never work!"

Oh but it did, didn't it? And how! On Tuesday morning I woke to the sound of a herd of wild pigs rampaging round the bathroom. Or at least that's what the terrible grunting and shrieking coming from the bathroom, sounded like.

"Look at this!" Dad yelled, swinging round from the mirror, as I burst in.

I had to laugh. I couldn't help it. Three dark, bushy tufts of hair were sticking up from his otherwise bald head. I honestly thought he'd stuck them there for a joke.

"I can't go to work like this!" he yelled, bringing Kerry rushing in. "I look ridiculous!"

"Quit panicking, Dad," said Kerry, practical as always. "Just shave it off."

By then, Dad was in a bit of a hurry and ended up with a couple of nasty scratches zig-zagging across his head, but otherwise the shaver did the trick. Or seemed to.

That night, I was surprised when Dad arrived home about half an hour after us. He teaches at a school about ten miles away and, by the time he's finished with meetings and after-school clubs, he's rarely home before half past six.

Even more surprised when me and Kerry looked up from our homework to see Dad hovering over us wearing a stupid, woolly hat pulled down, right over his forehead.

"Well, I had to wear something, didn't I?" he said. "Dug it out of the lost property box at break and I've been wearing it ever since because..."

I wondered what he could possibly be hiding that looked dafter than a turquoise hat with orange stripes and a purple bobble.

I didn't have long to wait. As he whipped off the hat, masses of red hair tumbled out onto his shoulders, over his face.

I laughed. Kerry screamed. Dad threw his bag onto the floor, took off his jacket, loosened his tie and flopped into a chair.

"What have you done?" wailed Kerry. "I mean, have you been slapping that stuff all over your face and chest as well?"

Dad looked down to where bundles of dark hair were thrusting out of his

shirt, seeming to grow even as we watched.

"No," he said, scratching his chin, which was beginning to sprout a little beard. "Just my head. It's ridiculous! I don't understand it."

"Go and get the bottle, Max," said Kerry in her bossy, irritating way. "And let's have a look. Maybe Dad didn't read the instructions properly."

"What instructions?" said Dad. "There weren't any instructions."

"Yes, there were," I said, when I'd rescued the bottle from the bathroom bin. "On the back of the label."

"Stupid place to put instructions," Dad muttered, as I peeled off the label and began to read.

"Squeeze one drop onto the scalp and rub in thoroughly. WARNING: NEVER USE MORE THAN THREE DROPS IN TWENTY-FOUR HOURS."

"Er, Dad," said Kerry, snatching the bottle and tipping it upside down. "How much did you use exactly?"

CHAPTER 4

"All of it," said Dad. "I used all of it."

"All of it!" shrieked Kerry.

"Well, it was really thick," said Dad. "Not like a liquid at all. So I just slapped it on and left it for twenty minutes while I had my bath."

"I think I'd better phone the doctor," said Kerry.

"No," said Dad, hastily. "It's not as if I'm ill, exactly, is it? Besides, his kids go to my school and I'm not taking the risk of this getting out, no way! I'll just have to keep shaving until it wears off."

Shaving! We blunted two pairs of scissors, got through a dozen razor blades and filled a bin liner full of hair that night! But we won, in the end. His face was smooth, his head was smooth and his legs and chest were no hairier than usual.

It took ages and I have to admit I felt a bit guilty, even though it was his own stupid fault for not reading the instructions. So, on Wednesday morning, I took him breakfast in bed. Just to make it up to him a bit.

I pushed open the door and leaned against the light switch, all the time carefully balancing the tray in both hands.

"Uuuh," groaned the shape under the duvet. "What time is it?"

"Quarter to..."

The words froze in my mouth and the tray started to tremble in my hands as the cover was thrown back and a faceless, shaggy beast began to emerge.

I knew it was my dad. I knew that however wild the creature looked, it wasn't going to hurt me. But it didn't help. It really didn't help.

It was Dad who screamed first

though, I swear. It was Dad who made the tray shoot out of my hand, raining down a deluge of toast, tea, milk and Rice Krispies on top of him.

By the time Kerry arrived, the hot tea had soaked through his fur and onto his skin, so he was hopping around yelping, brushing Krispies off his milk-splattered, hairy arms.

No way could we cut and shave that lot off in time for him to get to work, so that's when Kerry phoned in and told them he'd broken his leg. A broken leg, I ask you! Couldn't she have said a cold or something?

Anyway, Dad wouldn't hear of us taking the day off too, so we left him snipping fur off his feet and went to school.

Not that I could concentrate. It was beginning to dawn on me that the damage might be permanent. That my

poor dad might have to spend the rest of his days as a freak. That he'd lose his job!

I mean, I know it's all equal opportunities these days, but no one's going to want their kids taught by something straight out of *Planet of the Apes,* now, are they?

I couldn't wait to get home. Hoping and praying that he'd be back to normal.

He wasn't. In fact, if anything, he was hairier than ever.

"You might have at least tried to cut it a bit," moaned Kerry.

"Cut it?" said Dad, leading us into the kitchen. "Cut it! Look at that!"

Five black bin liners were propped up against various surfaces. And they were all full of hair.

"What am I going to do with that lot?" he asked.

"Knit a jumper?" I suggested. "Make a nice rug?"

"It's not funny, Max," said Dad, looking really distressed. "The more I cut, the more it seems to grow. What am I going to do?"

"We ought to phone Futurama," said Kerry. "See if they've got any suggestions."

"We can't," I said. "I've told you. I've lost the catalogue."

"I'm not surprised," said Kerry, heading for my bedroom. "The state of this place!"

Kerry found the catalogue under a pile of dirty football socks, under my bed. But it didn't help.

"They don't give a phone number," she said. "Or an e-address."

"Well, there's a postal address," said Dad. "So maybe we could get the number from directory enquiries."

"I don't think so," said Kerry. "PO Box 7, Milton Keynes. That's all it says."

"Are you sure?" I asked, snatching the catalogue from her.

"We'll have to write, then," said Dad, looking at his hairy hands.

"Wait a minute," I said, as Kerry grabbed a note-pad. "Hang on. I think I've found something."

"Are you mad?" Kerry yelled, as I showed her my great find.

"Makes sense," I said. "If *Dr Hepplewaite's Hair Restorer* caused the problem, then maybe his hair remover could solve it."

"Funny idea of sense, you've got," Kerry muttered. "And that flaming catalogue's caused enough problems as it is. I reckon it's time Dad saw a proper doctor."

"No!" said Dad. "I think Max might be right. It's worth a try. If we can sort this out without anyone ever knowing. Write a note, Kerry. Tell them the problem. Tell them it's URGENT. How many bottles do you think we'll need?"

He sent for thirty, just to be on the safe side. Thirty bottles at £9.99 each! Nearly £300. But Dad said it would be worth every penny *IF* it worked.

CHAPTER 6

Only before it could work, it had to arrive, didn't it? We posted the cheque that Wednesday night, but by Saturday, nothing had turned up. By the following Tuesday, still nothing.

We'd filled another twenty bags of hair and Dad was getting decidedly grumpy. Especially when one of the teachers from his school popped round that evening to see how he was.

"You can't see him," Kerry said,

refusing to open the door more than a centimetre. "He's asleep. He's in a lot of pain. From the broken leg. Might not be back for months!"

"What did you tell him that for?" Dad groaned, when Kerry had finally got rid of him. "I've got to get back soon, or I'll need a sick note. How am I supposed to fake a broken leg? How am I going to get rid of all this hair? What am I going to do?"

Well, I couldn't really blame Dad for feeling a bit fed up. But all he had to do was wait. I was sure the hair remover would work, when it turned up. If it turned up. But him going on his little ramble that night didn't help, did it?

No way could I get back to sleep after Mrs Burrow's hysterics. I lay awake for the rest of the night, wondering what on earth we were going to do.

"Has the post been yet?" I asked
Kerry on the Wednesday morning,
after Dad had already been off work a
whole week.

"Yes."

"And?" I asked, eagerly.

"A gas bill, a phone bill and a letter
from Gran."

"Oh. So, er, how's Dad?"

"Hairy," Kerry said.
"And a bit manic."

Poor Dad had so
much hair by then,
he could barely get
any clothes on. Just
his old swimming
shorts with the
loose string.

"Whatever you
do," I told him, "don't
go out, and keep away
from the window!"

"Maybe it'll come tomorrow," Kerry said, hopefully, as we left for school.

But it was already getting worse than I could have ever imagined.

"There's been another monkey-man sighting," Nick Leech yelled out of his bedroom window. "My mum saw it, at 5 o'clock this morning. When she set off for early shift."

"She couldn't have done," Kerry whispered to me. "Dad didn't go out again. I know he didn't. He wouldn't have."

By the end of the day, Kerry wasn't so sure.

"Three people in my class reckon they know someone who's seen it," she hissed.

"Danny Fairbrother, in my class, says he saw it too, rummaging in his dustbin," I told her.

"Maybe it's worse than we

thought," said Kerry. "Maybe it's effected Dad's brain or something. Maybe he's going out and he doesn't even realise it!"

"No way!" I said. "It's just people making it up, isn't it? You know what it's like. Give people the hint of a juicy story and they all want in on it. It's a sort of mass hysteria. Like all the people who reckon they see spaceships and aliens."

"I hope so," said Kerry shuddering. "Because one or two people have reported pet rabbits and cats going missing. And, after what Brenda Burrows said last night about it chasing her terrier..."

"Oh, for goodness sake," I said. "You're not telling me Dad's taken to eating cats, now, are you?"

Still, it gave me a nasty turn when we couldn't find Marmalade when we got home. Especially with Dad sitting there, snipping away with the garden shears!

Fortunately, Marmalade turned up after an hour or two and we didn't tell Dad about the rumours. We thought he had enough to worry about with his headmaster on the phone, hassling him about when he was going to send his sick note in.

"It's no good," said Dad, hanging his hairy head in despair. "If the stuff doesn't come tomorrow, I'll have to call the doctor. See what he can do."

It was agony. We had to leave for school before the postman had been and spend the day listening to increasingly bizarre rumours.

"My brother reckons it might have escaped from that lab," Danny Fairbrother said. "You know...where they do those experiments."

Meaning the cosmetics company, fifty miles away, that stopped doing tests on animals about ten years ago!

"It broke into my grandad's hen-house last night," Nina Marconi said. "Killed three chickens. There were feathers and blood everywhere."

Everyone gawped at her, open-mouthed. Taking it all in. Didn't seem to occur to anybody that it was probably just a fox!

I was desperate to get home, but I hung around for ten minutes, waiting for Kerry to come out of senior school, like I always do. And, as luck would have it, old Mr Peters pulled up to give us a lift on his way back from his weekly shopping trip.

"There's an article about our monkey-man in the local paper," he said, as he pottered along at fifteen miles an hour. "Page six. Have a look if you like."

I could hear Kerry rustling the newspaper in the back.

"Monkey-man mystery," she read.

"Dozens of people in the Farleton area have reported sightings of a huge, hairy creature, said to be over eight-foot tall."

"He's grown a bit," I muttered.

"All those cats he's been eating," laughed Kerry.

"It's not funny, young lady," said Mr Peters, slowing down to ten miles an hour as a police car raced past and swung into our road.

"Oh no," said Kerry. "Oh no!"

CHAPTER 7

It seemed like hours before Mr Peters pulled up behind the police car, which had parked next to the Parcel Post van outside our house, but I guess it was only a couple of minutes.

I recognised the young policewoman who'd been there on Tuesday night. She was on her own, this time, apart from Mrs Burrows and a bloke with a Parcel Post badge on his shirt.

"It's in your house," Brenda squealed

at us as we got out of the car. "It's in your house. I saw it. And your poor, defenceless dad laid up with a broken leg and all."

"It's all right," said the policewoman, putting her arm round Kerry who'd turned absolutely white. "I'm sure your daddy will be fine. I'm sending for extra help."

"This is ridiculous," I said, trying to sound more confident than I felt. "There's nothing in there. It was probably just Dad she saw, hobbling around."

"No way was that your dad," said Brenda. "Ask him," she added, pointing at the postal worker. "Go on. Ask him. He saw it."

"I had a parcel to deliver," the man said, as Kerry and I looked at each other. "And when I rang the door bell, this voice yells at me to leave the parcel on the step. Well, I can't, can I? 'Cos it has to be signed for, doesn't it? But, as I'm trying to explain this, your neighbour comes out and offers to take it."

"She would!" I mumbled.

"So, I'm looking at her, when your door opens and something snatches the parcel right out of my hands and slams the door."

"So you didn't exactly see who it was?" said Kerry.

"Er, not exactly but..."

"See!" I said. "It was Dad."

"Surely your father wouldn't just snatch a parcel, like that?" said the policewoman.

"He might," said Kerry. "He hasn't been, er, quite himself, recently. It's the pain. From his leg."

"That was NOT your dad," screeched Brenda. "Not unless he's suddenly grown a six-foot beard."

Close. Definitely, frighteningly close. And I was just wondering how on earth we were going to get inside to hide him, before the whole of the emergency services descended, when our front door started to open.

Brenda screamed. The postal worker gasped. But the policewoman was made of sterner stuff. She marched

71

forward with me and Kerry behind her.

This was it, then. The game was up. At best, Dad would be a laughing stock. At worst he'd be arrested for terrorising the neighbourhood, murdering cats and all the other terrible things monkey-man had been accused of.

I squeezed past the policewoman and there, standing in the doorway, was Dad.

He was looking dead cool in his black shirt and black jeans, with the sun glinting off the top of his bald, shiny head. Strangely, his eyebrows were missing, but he didn't look too bad without them.

"Dad!" Kerry shouted. "Are you all right? Only Mrs Burrows thought she saw that awful monkey-man INSIDE our house!"

"Oh," said Dad. "Er, did she? Well, that's strange. I mean, I've been busy catching up on a bit of paperwork, but

I'm sure I'd have noticed a seven foot ape-man loping around."

"And did you take a parcel from the postman?" asked the policewoman.

"Yes," said Dad, smiling. "I was on the loo when the doorbell rang. I've had a bit of a tummy bug. So I just grabbed the parcel and darted back to the loo. Then I realised I hadn't signed for it, which is why I came back out."

Quick thinking, eh? I told you Dad was quite smart, didn't I? And his story sounded fine to me, so why was the policewoman looking at him all sort of funny?

"Tummy bug?" she said. "I thought you had a broken leg?"

"Oh, no!" said Dad, smiling again. "Just a nasty sprain. It's a lot better now. In fact, I would have been back at work today, if it hadn't been for the bug."

Honestly, cops are so suspicious.

The policewoman was still looking at him funny. Then, I realised. It wasn't a suspicious look. It was a soppy look. And it took her a second or two to pull herself together.

"Right," she said, as Mrs Burrows stomped off. "Well, everything seems to be in order. But I wonder if you'd mind me popping in and doing a quick check."

"No, not at all," said Dad, calmly.

He led the way, hobbling with a wildly exaggerated limp, before turning to us.

"But I think you two had better go and clean up the dreadful mess you left in the bathroom this morning. I mean, as if I'm going to clean up after you with a sprained ankle."

"I didn't leave any m—" I started to say, as Kerry grabbed my arm and dragged me upstairs.

Mess, of course, turned out to be a

bit of an understatement. Torn cardboard and thirty empty bottles of *Dr Hepplewaite's Miracle Hair Remover* thrown everywhere. And the bath positively afloat with dark hair and yellow gunge. Yuk!

Spending half an hour cleaning up was a small price to pay for Dad's recovery, though. And, when we went

downstairs, the policewoman seemed in no hurry to do her check. Her and Dad were drinking tea and chatting as if they'd known each other for years.

Funnily enough, although Dad's wild hair didn't grow back, sightings of monkey-man went on for weeks after that. Which either means that people have incredibly vivid imaginations or that some other idiot who can't read instructions, has tried *Dr Hepplewaite's Miracle Hair Restorer*!

Dad actually confessed the truth to Amy, the policewoman, after they'd been out together a few times, but I don't think she believed him.

"He's a laugh, your dad, isn't he?" she said.

Amy doesn't seem to be at all put off by Dad's baldness and we all get on really well together so...

"It's early days yet, Max," Kerry said,

when I told her what I was thinking. "So don't get your hopes up. It might not come to anything."

"I know," I said. "But I'm glad I kept the Futurama catalogue."

"Why?"

"Well, if it does work out, I might be able to find them a really unusual wedding pres—"

"No, Max!" Kerry said. "Don't even think about it."